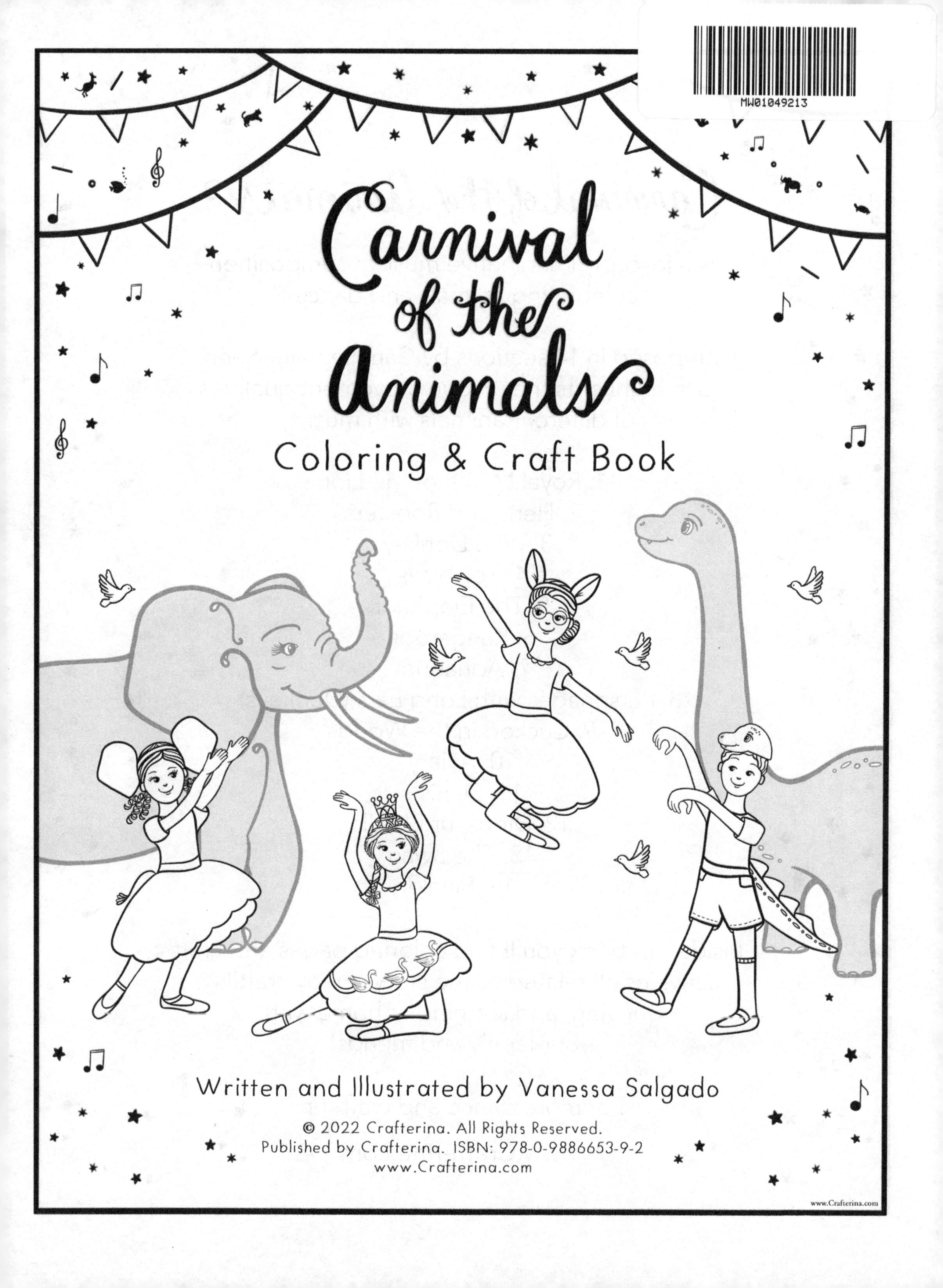
MW01049213
Carnival of the Animals
Coloring & Craft Book
Written and Illustrated by Vanessa Salgado
© 2022 Crafterina. All Rights Reserved.
Published by Crafterina. ISBN: 978-0-9886653-9-2
www.Crafterina.com
www.Crafterina.com

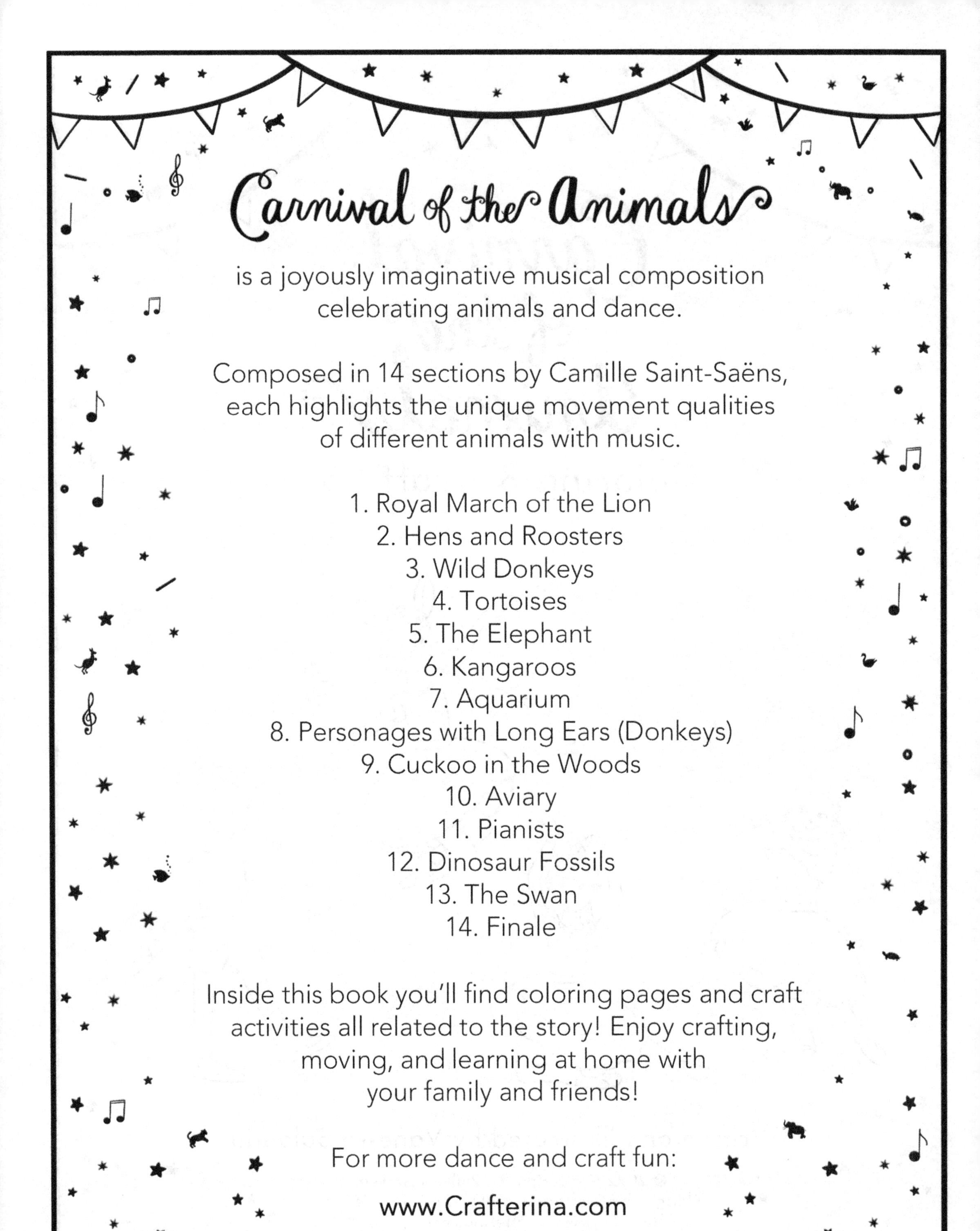

Carnival of the Animals

is a joyously imaginative musical composition
celebrating animals and dance.

Composed in 14 sections by Camille Saint-Saëns,
each highlights the unique movement qualities
of different animals with music.

1. Royal March of the Lion
2. Hens and Roosters
3. Wild Donkeys
4. Tortoises
5. The Elephant
6. Kangaroos
7. Aquarium
8. Personages with Long Ears (Donkeys)
9. Cuckoo in the Woods
10. Aviary
11. Pianists
12. Dinosaur Fossils
13. The Swan
14. Finale

Inside this book you'll find coloring pages and craft
activities all related to the story! Enjoy crafting,
moving, and learning at home with
your family and friends!

For more dance and craft fun:

www.Crafterina.com

Let's use our imaginations to dance like different animals!
www.Crafterina.com

Lion
www.Crafterina.com

Dancing Lion
www.Crafterina.com

Hens and Rooster
www.Crafterina.com

Dancing Hen and Rooster
www.Crafterina.com

Wild Donkeys
www.Crafterina.com

Wild Donkeys
www.Crafterina.com

Tortoise
www.Crafterina.com

Dancing
Tortoise
www.Crafterina.com

Elephant
www.Crafterina.com

Dancing
Elephants
www.Crafterina.com

Kangaroo
www.Crafterina.com

Dancing
Kangaroo
www.Crafterina.com

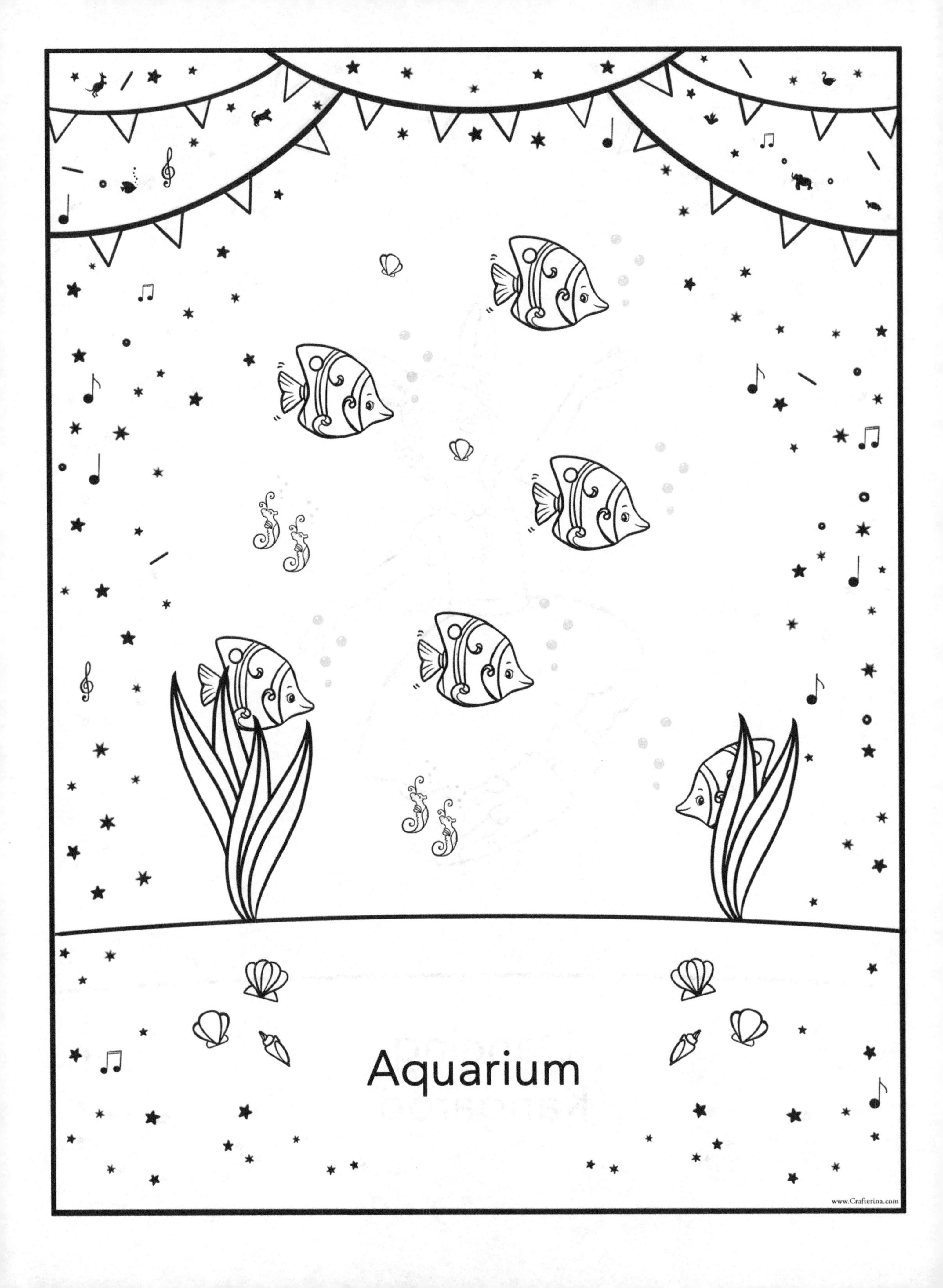
Aquarium
www.Crafterina.com

Dancing
Aquarium
www.Crafterina.com

Pianist
www.Crafterina.com

Pianist
www.Crafterina.com

Cuckoo in the Woods
www.Crafterina.com

Dancing Cuckoo Bird
www.Crafterina.com

Aviary
www.Crafterina.com

Dancing Birds
www.Crafterina.com

Dinosaur
www.Crafterina.com

Dancing
Dinosaur
www.Crafterina.com

Swan
www.Crafterina.com

Dancing Swans
www.Crafterina.com

Finale

Finale
www.Crafterina.com

Learn Animal Dances!
March proudly like a Lion
Reach high like an Elephant
Walk like a Rooster
www.Crafterina.com

Learn Animal Dances!
Move
big
like
a
Dinosaur
Move
gracefully
like a Swan
www.Crafterina.com

Learn Animal Dances!
Move as fast
as a Bird
Kick backwards
like a Donkey
Move as slow
as a Tortoise
www.Crafterina.com

Learn Animal Dances!
Fly like a Bird
Jump like a Kangaroo
Swim like a Fish in the Sea
www.Crafterina.com

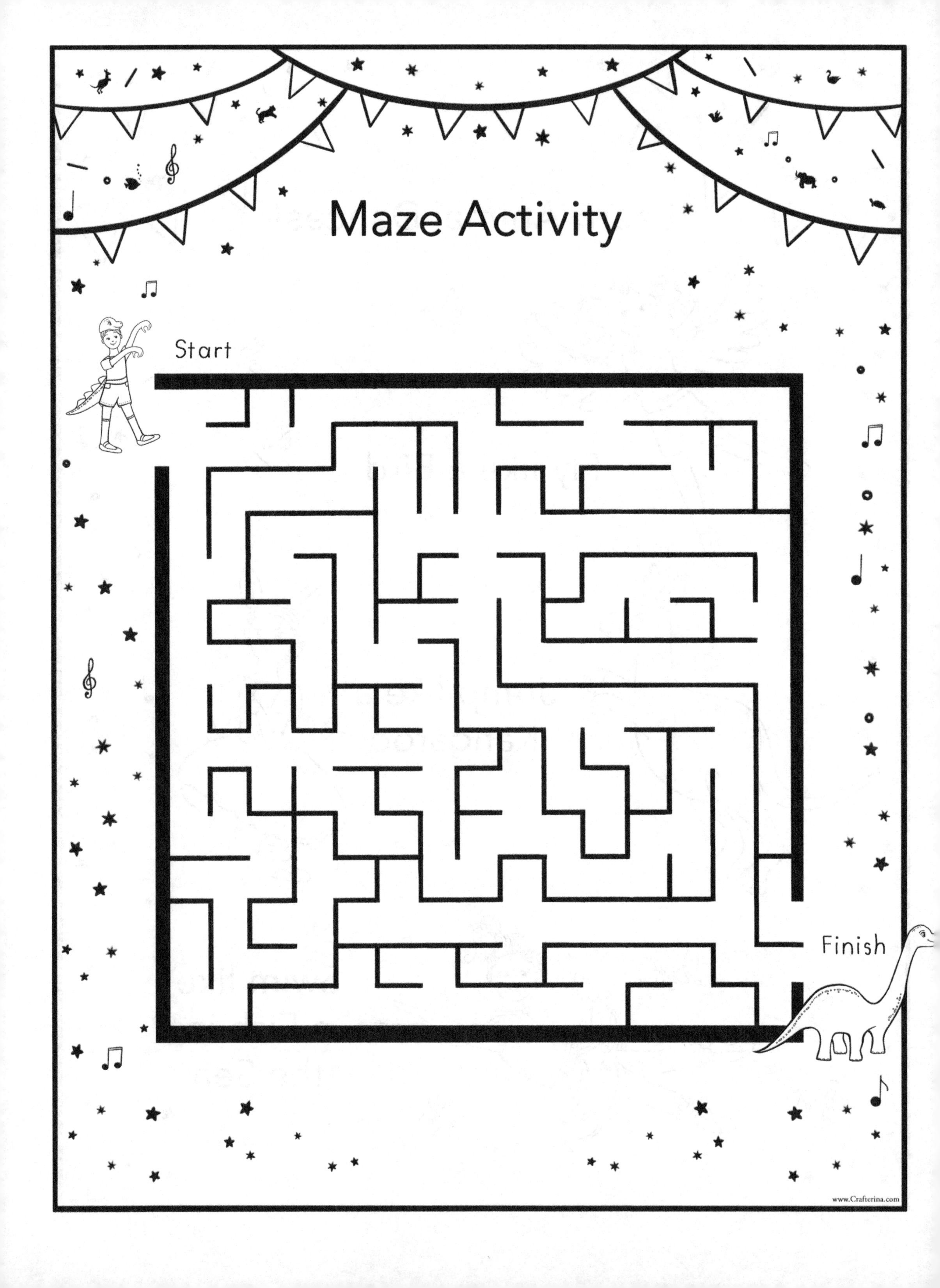
Maze Activity
Start
Finish
www.Crafterina.com

Matching Activity
Match each animal to the
correct set of footprints!
www.Crafterina.com

Matching Activity

Match each animal to the correct sound they make!

ROAR!

Hee-haw!

Cock-a-doodle-do!

Tweet-tweet!

Drawing Activity

Let's learn how to draw a Tortoise!

1.

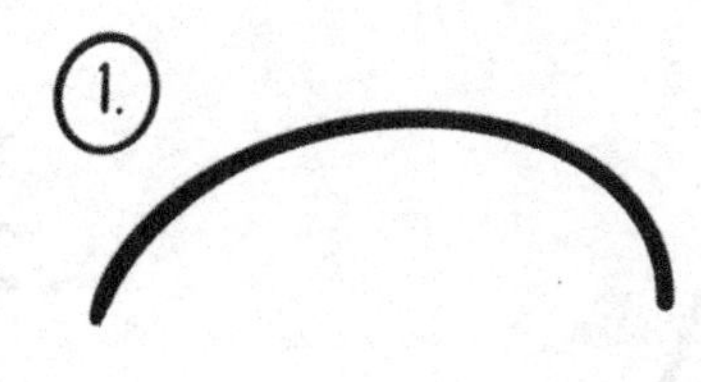

Draw half an oval

2.

Draw scallop lines to connect the shape

3.

Draw one long curve and small lines at scallop points

4.

Draw a head, neck and smile

5.

Add three small feet and a tail

6.

Add finishing touches! Draw an eye, brow, and nails!

Use this area to draw your own!

Carnival of the Animals

Let's create crafts!

Safety Note For Parents: These crafts require parent supervision to create. There are pieces to cut out and will require your help. Have fun creating together!

Crown

Party Hat

Paper Doll

Flashcards

Carnival of the Animals
Crown Paper Craft
Directions:
1.
Cut out crown template
2.
Connect ends with glue or tape to make ring
3.
Time to celebrate!
www.Crafterina.com

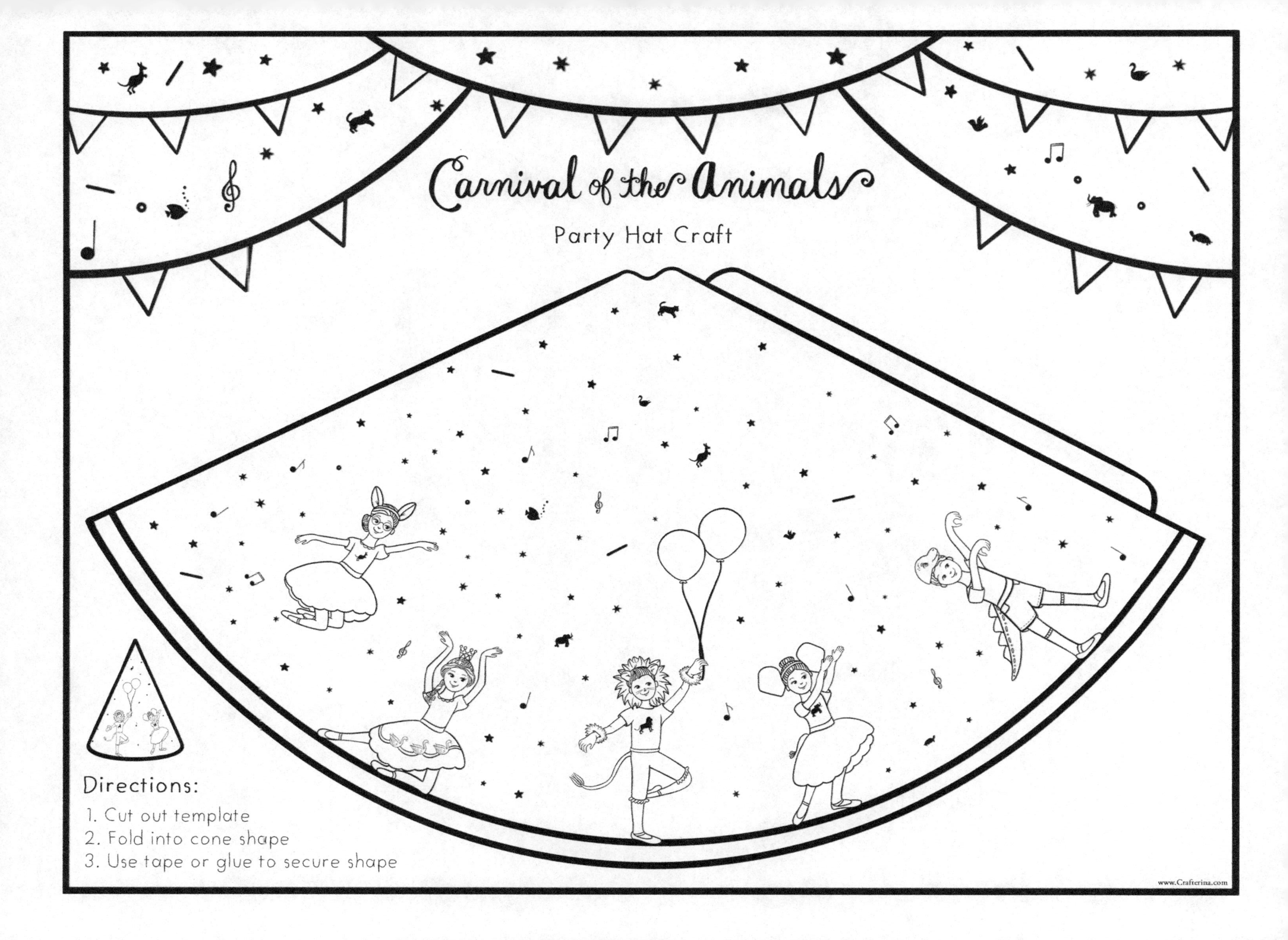
Carnival of the Animals
Party Hat Craft
Directions:
1. Cut out template
2. Fold into cone shape
3. Use tape or glue to secure shape
www.Crafterina.com

Carnival of the Animals
Animal Dance Flashcards

Swim

Reach

Jump

Kick

Fly

Walk

March

Play Animal Charades:

Pick a card and have a friend guess what animal you are as you dance

Choreography Activity:

Make your own dance by placing movement cards in different orders

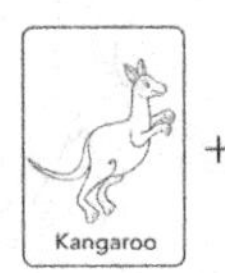

+

+

= Dance all three in a row to make your own phrase

Wild Donkey

Kangaroo

Elephant

Lion

Rooster

Bird

Move Slow

Move
Low

Dino Arms

Move
High

Flap
Arms

Fast Fingers

Move
Fast

WILD CARD

Create
Your
Own
Animal
Dance

Carnival of the Animals
Paper Doll Craft
www.Crafterina.com

About the Author

Vanessa Salgado is a Professional Dancer, Educator and Illustrator.

She has taught many little dancers across Manhattan, concentrating primarily at the Joffrey Ballet School, School at STEPS on Broadway, and Alvin Ailey School. She has also worked as an Associate for the Education Department at New York City Center. Vanessa is a graduate of the Alvin Ailey/Fordham University BFA Program at Lincoln Center and holds a certification in Dance Education. Her work has been featured in Dance Teacher Magazine, Dance Spirit, Dance Informa, and METRO US Newspaper, among others.

Her earliest memories involve story time with her dad, creating with her mom after school, and attending weekend ballet class alongside her sister, Donna. Her interests in visual art blossomed in high school as she simultaneously trained for the professional dance world. As she transitioned from her college days into professional life, her incessant doodles and crafting have remained a source of wonder for all those around her.

For more information:
www.VanessaSalgado.com

About Crafterina®

Vanessa is also the creator of Crafterina® a series of dance education books and crafts for families. Designed to spark imagination and inspire movement at home, Crafterina® uniquely incorporates reading, creating and dancing in one. Through this interdisciplinary approach, Crafterina® playfully encourages empowerment and teaches youngsters they have the ability to make anything possible.

Inspire a lifelong love for learning in dance with the help of Crafterina®.

For more information, visit our website for books, crafts, and printables:

www.Crafterina.com

Crafterina®

ABCs of
Classical Ballet
Written and Illustrated by Vanessa Salgado
with Donna Salgado

ABCs of
Animal Dances
Written and Illustrated by Vanessa Salgado
with Donna Salgado

Nutcracker
Coloring & Craft Book
A Crafterina® Book
Written and Illustrated
by Vanessa Salgado

Ballerina Party
Coloring & Craft Book
Written and Illustrated
by Vanessa Salgado
A Crafterina® Book

Made in the USA
Monee, IL
07 April 2025

15369722R00031